Out of the Dust

*Also by Karen Hesse
in Large Print:*

Stowaway

Out of the Dust

KAREN HESSE

Thorndike Press • Waterville, Maine

Recommended for Middle Readers.

Copyright © 1997 by Karen Hesse.

Published in 2004 by arrangement with Scholastic, Inc.

Thorndike Press® Large Print The Literacy Bridge.

The tree indicium is a trademark of Thorndike Press.

The text of this Large Print edition is unabridged.
Other aspects of the book may vary from the original edition.

Set in 16 pt. Plantin by Liana M. Walker.

Printed in the United States on permanent paper.

Library of Congress Cataloging-in-Publication Data

Hesse, Karen.
    Out of the dust / Karen Hesse.
      p. cm.
      Summary: In a series of poems, fifteen-year-old Billie
Jo relates the hardships of living on her family's wheat
farm in Oklahoma during the dust bowl years of the
Depression.
    ISBN 0-7862-7006-3 (lg. print : hc : alk. paper)
    1. Large type books. [1. Dust storms — Fiction. 2. Farm
life — Oklahoma — Fiction. 3. Depressions — 1929 —
Fiction. 4. Oklahoma — History — 20th century —
Fiction. 5. Poetry — Fiction. 6. Large type books.]
I. Title.
PZ7.H4364Ou 2004
  [Fic]—dc22
                                  2004042303

To Brenda Bowen,
who is so much more than an editor

I extend heartfelt thanks to
Eileen Christelow,
Kate, Rachel, and Randy Hesse,
Liza Ketchum,
Jeffrey and Bernice Millman,
Maryann Sparks,
and the Oklahoma Historical Society.

Winter 1934

Beginning: August 1920

As summer wheat came ripe,
so did I,
born at home, on the kitchen floor.
Ma crouched,
barefoot, bare bottomed
over the swept boards,
because that's where Daddy said it'd be best.

I came too fast for the doctor,
bawling as soon as Daddy wiped
   his hand around
inside my mouth.
To hear Ma tell it,
I hollered myself red the day I was born.
Red's the color I've stayed ever since.

Daddy named me Billie Jo.
He wanted a boy.
Instead,
he got a long-legged girl
with a wide mouth
and cheekbones like bicycle handles.
He got a redheaded, freckle-faced,
   narrow-hipped girl
with a fondness for apples
and a hunger for playing fierce piano.

From the earliest I can remember
I've been restless in this
little Panhandle shack we call home,
always getting in Ma's way with my
pointy elbows, my fidgety legs.
By the summer I turned nine Daddy had
given up about having a boy.
He tried making me do.
I look just like him,
I can handle myself most everywhere
    he puts me,
even on the tractor,
though I don't like that much.

Ma tried having other babies.
It never seemed to go right, except with me.
But this morning
Ma let on as how she's expecting again.
Other than the three of us
there's not much family to speak of.
Daddy, the only boy Kelby left
since Grandpa died
from a cancer
that ate up the most of his skin,
and Aunt Ellis,
almost fourteen years older than Daddy
and living in Lubbock,
a ways south of here,
and a whole world apart
to hear Daddy tell it.

And Ma, with only Great-uncle Floyd,
old as ancient Indian bones,
and mean as a rattler,
rotting away in that room down in Dallas.

I'll be nearly fourteen
just like Aunt Ellis was when Daddy was born
by the time this baby comes.

Wonder if Daddy'll get his boy this time?

January 1934

Rabbit Battles

Mr. Noble and
Mr. Romney have a bet going
as to who can kill the most rabbits.
It all started at the rabbit drive last Monday
over to Sturgis
when Mr. Noble got himself worked up
about the damage done to his crop by jacks.
Mr. Romney swore he'd had
   more rabbit trouble
than anyone in Cimarron County.
They pledged revenge on
   the rabbit population;
wagering who could kill more.

They ought to just shut up.
Betting on how many rabbits they can kill.
Honestly!
Grown men clubbing bunnies to death.
Makes me sick to my stomach.
I know rabbits eat what they shouldn't,
especially this time of year
   when they could hop
halfway to Liberal
and still not find food,
but Miss Freeland says
if we keep

plowing under the stuff
   they ought to be eating,
what are they supposed to do?

Mr. Noble and
Mr. Romney came home
   from Sturgis Monday
with twenty rabbits apiece. A tie.
It should've stopped there. But
Mr. Romney wasn't satisfied.
He said,
"Noble cheated.
He brought in rabbits somebody else killed."
And so the contest goes on.

Those men,
they used to be best friends.
Now they can't be civil with each other.
They scowl as they pass on the street.
I'm scowling too,
but scowling won't bring the rabbits back.
They're all skinned and cooked
   and eaten by now.
At least they didn't end up in
Romney and Noble's cook pots.
They went to families
that needed the meat.

January 1934

Losing Livie

Livie Killian moved away.
I didn't want her to go.
We'd been friends since first grade.

The farewell party was
Thursday night
at the Old Rock Schoolhouse.

Livie
had something to tease each of us about,
like Ray
sleeping through reading class,
and Hillary,
who on her speed-writing test put
an "even ton" of children
instead of an "even ten."

Livie said good-bye to each of us,
separately.
She gave me a picture she'd made
    of me sitting
in front of a piano,
wearing my straw hat,
an apple halfway to my mouth.

I handed Livie the memory book we'd all

filled with our different slants.
I couldn't get the muscles
   in my throat relaxed enough
to tell her how much I'd miss her.

Livie
helped clean up her own party,
wiping spilled lemonade,
gathering sandwich crusts,
sweeping cookie crumbs from the floor,
while the rest of us went home
to study for semester reviews.

Now Livie's gone west,
out of the dust,
on her way to California,
where the wind takes a rest sometimes.
And I'm wondering
   what kind of friend I am,
wanting my feet on that road
   to another place,
instead of Livie's.

January 1934

15

Me and Mad Dog

Arley Wanderdale,
who teaches music once a week
   at our school,
though Ma says he's no teacher at all,
just a local song plugger,
Arley Wanderdale asked
if I'd like to play a piano solo
at the Palace Theatre on Wednesday night.

I grinned,
pleased to be asked, and said,
"That'd be all right."

I didn't know if Ma would let me.
She's an old mule on the subject
   of my schooling.
She says,
"You stay home on weeknights, Billie Jo."
And mostly that's what I do.

But Arley Wanderdale said,
"The management asked me to
bring them talent, Billie Jo,
and I thought of you."

Even before Mad Dog Craddock?
   I wondered.
"You and Mad Dog,"
   Arley Wanderdale said.

Darn that blue-eyed boy
with his fine face and his
smooth voice,
twice as good
as a plowboy has any right to be.
I suspected Mad Dog had come first
to Arley Wanderdale's mind,
but I didn't get too riled.
Not so riled I couldn't say yes.

January 1934

Permission to Play

Sometimes,
when Ma is busy in the kitchen,
or scrubbing,
or doing wash,
I can ask her something in such a way
I annoy her just enough to get an answer,
but not so much I get a no.

That's a way I've found of gaining
    what I want,
by catching Ma off guard,
especially when I'm after permission
    to play piano.
Right out asking her is no good.
She always gets testy about me playing,
even though she's the one
    who truly taught me.

Anyway, this time I caught her in the
slow stirring of biscuits,
her mind on other things,
maybe the baby growing inside her,
    I don't know,
but anyhow,
she was distracted enough,
I was determined enough,

this time I got just what I wanted. Permission to play at the Palace.

January 1934

On Stage

When I point my fingers at the keys,
    the music
springs straight out of me.
    Right hand
playing notes sharp as
    tongues,
telling stories while the
    smooth
buttery rhythms back me up
    on the left.

Folks sway in the
    Palace aisles
grinning and stomping and
    out of breath,
and the rest, eyes shining,
    fingers snapping,
feet tapping. It's the best
    I've ever felt,
playing hot piano,
    sizzling with
Mad Dog,
    swinging with the Black Mesa Boys,
or on my own,
    crazy,
pestering the keys.

That is
heaven.
How supremely
heaven
playing piano
can be.

January 1934

Birthday for F.D.R.

I played so well
on Wednesday night,
Arley put his arm across my shoulder
and asked me to come and
perform at the President's birthday ball.
Ma can't say no to this one.
It's for President Roosevelt.
Not that Mr. Roosevelt
    will actually be there,
but the money collected at the ball,
along with balls all over the country,
will go,
in the President's name,
to the Warm Springs Foundation,
where Mr. Roosevelt stayed once
    when he was sick.

Someday,
I plan to play for
    President Franklin Delano Roosevelt
himself.
Maybe I'll go all the way
    to the White House in
Washington, D.C.
In the meantime,
it's pretty nice

Arley asking me to play twice,
for Joyce City.

January 1934

Not Too Much To Ask

We haven't had a good crop in three years,
not since the bounty of '31,
and we're all whittled down
   to the bone these days,
even Ma, with her new round belly,
but still
when the committee came asking,
Ma donated:
three jars of apple sauce
and
some cured pork,
and a
feed-sack nightie she'd sewn
   for our coming baby.

February 1934

Mr. Hardly's Money Handling

It was Daddy's birthday
and Ma decided to bake him a cake.
There wasn't
money enough for anything
   like a real present.
Ma sent me to fetch the extras
with fifty cents she'd been hiding away.
"Don't go to Joyce City, Billie," she said.
"You can get what we need
   down Hardly's store."

I slipped the coins into my sweater pocket,
   the pocket
without the hole,
thinking about how many sheets
   of new music
fifty cents would buy.

Mr. Hardly glared
when the Wonder Bread door
banged shut behind me.
He squinted as I creaked
   across the wooden floor.
Mr. Hardly was in the habit
of charging too much for his stale food,
and he made bad change when he thought

he could get away with it.
I squinted back at him
    as I gave him Ma's order.

Mr. Hardly's
been worse than normal
since his attic filled with dust
and collapsed under the weight.
He hired folks for the repairs,
and argued over every nail and every
little minute.
The whole place took
shoveling for days before he could
open again and
some stock was so bad it
had to be thrown away.

The stove clanked in the corner
as Mr. Hardly filled Ma's order.
I could smell apples,
ground coffee, and peppermint.
I sorted through the patterns
    on the feed bags,
sneezed dust,
blew my nose.

When Mr. Hardly finished
    sacking my things,
I paid the bill,
and tucking the list in my pocket

along with the change,
hurried home,
so Ma could bake the cake
    before Daddy came in.

But after Ma emptied the sack,
setting each packet out on the
oilcloth, she counted her change
and I remembered with a sinking feeling
that I hadn't kept an eye on
Mr. Hardly's money handling,
and Mr. Hardly had cheated again.
Only this time he'd cheated himself,
    giving us
four cents extra.

So while Ma mixed a cake,
I walked back to Mr. Hardly's store,
back through the dust,
back through the Wonder Bread door,
and thinking about the secondhand music
in a moldy box at the shop in Joyce City,
music I could have for two cents a sheet,
I placed Mr. Hardly's overpayment
    on the counter
and turned to head back home.

Mr. Hardly cleared his throat and
I wondered for a moment
if he'd call me back to offer

a piece of peppermint
or pick me out an apple from the crate,
but he didn't,
and that's okay.
Ma would have thrown a fit
if I'd taken a gift from him.

February 1934

Fifty Miles South of Home

In Amarillo,
wind
blew plate-glass windows in,
tore electric signs down,
ripped wheat
straight out of the ground.

February 1934

Rules of Dining

Ma has rules for setting the table.
I place plates upside down,
glasses bottom side up,
napkins folded over forks,
    knives, and spoons.

When dinner is ready,
we sit down together
and Ma says,
"Now."

We shake out our napkins,
spread them on our laps,
and flip over our glasses and plates,
exposing neat circles,
round comments
on what life would be without dust.

Daddy says,
"The potatoes are peppered
    plenty tonight, Polly,"
and
"Chocolate milk for dinner,
    aren't we in clover!"
when really all our pepper and chocolate,
it's nothing but dust.

I heard word from Livie Killian.
The Killians can't find work,
can't get food.
Livie's brother, Reuben, fifteen last summer,
took off, thinking to make it on his own.
I hope he's okay.

With a baby growing inside Ma,
it scares me thinking,
    Where would we be without
somewhere to live?
Without some work to do?
Without something to eat?
At least we've got milk.
    Even if we have to chew it.

February 1934

Breaking Drought

After seventy days
of wind and sun,
of wind and clouds,
of wind and sand,
after seventy days,
of wind and dust,
a little
rain
came.

February 1934

Dazzled

In the kitchen she is my ma,
in the barn and the fields
    she is my daddy's wife,
but in the parlor Ma is something different.
She isn't much to look at,
so long and skinny,
her teeth poor,
her dark hair always needing a wash, but
from the time I was four,
I remember being dazzled by her
whenever she played the piano.

Daddy bought it, an old Cramer,
his wedding gift to her.
She came to this house and
    found gaps in the walls,
a rusty bed, no running water,
and that piano,
gleaming in the corner.

Daddy gets soft eyes,
    standing behind her while she
plays.
I want someone to look that way at me.

On my fifth birthday,
Ma sat me down beside her
and started me to reading music,
started me to playing.
I'm not half so good as Ma.
She can pull Daddy into the parlor
even after the last milking, when he's so beat
he barely knows his own name
and all he wants
is a mattress under his bones.
You've got to be something
to get his notice that time of day,
but Ma can.
I'm not half so good with my crazy playing
as she is with her fine tunes and her
fancy fingerwork.
But I'm good enough for Arley, I guess.

March 1934

Debts

Daddy is thinking
of taking a loan from Mr. Roosevelt
  and his men,
to get some new wheat planted
where the winter crop
  has spindled out and died.
Mr. Roosevelt promises
Daddy won't have to pay a dime
till the crop comes in.

Daddy says,
"I can turn the fields over,
start again.
It's sure to rain soon.
Wheat's sure to grow."

Ma says, "What if it doesn't?"

Daddy takes off his hat,
roughs up his hair,
puts the hat back on.
"Course it'll rain," he says.

Ma says, "Bay,
it hasn't rained enough to grow wheat in
three years."

Daddy looks like a fight brewing.
He takes that red face of his out to the barn,
to keep from feuding with my pregnant ma.

I ask Ma
how,
after all this time,
Daddy still believes in rain.

"Well, it rains enough," Ma says,
"now and again,
to keep a person hoping.
But even if it didn't
your daddy would have to believe.
It's coming on spring,
and he's a farmer."

March 1934

Foul as Maggoty Stew

Arley Wanderdale said
the rehearsals for *Sunny of Sunnyside*
shouldn't take me out of school
more than twice next week.

When I told Ma she got angry about
my missing school to play piano
    for some show.

Me and Daddy,
we're trying our best to please Ma,
for fear of what it might do to the baby
    if we don't.
I don't know why she's
so against my playing.
She says that school is important,
but I do all right in school.
I know she doesn't like the kind
of music I play,
but sometimes I think she's
just plain jealous
when I'm at the piano
and she's not.
And maybe she's a little afraid
of me going somewhere with the music
she can't follow.

Or of the music taking me
so far away one day
I'll never come home.
Whatever the reason,
   she said I couldn't do it.
Arley had to get somebody to take my place.

I do as she says. I go to school,
and in the afternoons I come home,
run through my chores,
do my reading and my math work at the
kitchen table
and all the while I glare at Ma's back
   with a scowl
foul as maggoty stew.

March 1934

State Tests

When I got home I told Ma
our school scored higher than the
whole state on achievement tests and
I scored top of eighth grade.

Ma nodded.
"I knew you could."

That's all she said.

She was proud,
I could tell.
But she didn't
coo like Mad Dog's ma. Or
go on
like Mrs. Killian used to do.
Daddy says,
"That's not your ma's way."
But I wish it was.
I wish she'd give me a little more
    to hold on to than
"I knew you could."
Instead she makes me feel like she's just
taking me in like I was
so much flannel dry on the line.

March 1934

Fields of Flashing Light

I heard the wind rise,
and stumbled from my bed,
down the stairs,
out the front door,
into the yard.
The night sky kept flashing,
lightning danced down on its spindly legs.

I sensed it before I knew it was coming.
I heard it,
smelled it,
tasted it.
Dust.

While Ma and Daddy slept,
the dust came,
tearing up fields where the winter wheat,
set for harvest in June,
stood helpless.
I watched the plants,
surviving after so much drought
  and so much wind,
I watched them fry,
or
flatten,
or blow away,

like bits of cast-off rags.
It wasn't until the dust turned
    toward the house,
like a fired locomotive,
and I fled,
barefoot and breathless, back inside,
it wasn't until the dust
hissed against the windows,
until it ratcheted the roof,
that Daddy woke.

He ran into the storm,
his overalls half-hooked over his union suit.
"Daddy!" I called. "You can't stop dust."

Ma told me to
cover the beds,
push the scatter rugs against the doors,
dampen the rags around the windows.
Wiping dust out of everything,
she made coffee and biscuits,
waiting for Daddy to come in.

Sometime after four,
rubbing low on her back,
Ma sank down into a chair
    at the kitchen table
and covered her face.
Daddy didn't come back for hours,
not

until the temperature dropped so low,
it brought snow.
Ma and I sighed, grateful,
staring out at the dirty flakes,
but our relief didn't last.
The wind snatched that snow
   right off the fields,
leaving behind a sea of dust,
waves and
waves and
waves of
dust,
rippling across our yard.

Daddy came in,
he sat across from Ma and blew his nose.
Mud streamed out.
He coughed and spit out
mud.
If he had cried,
his tears would have been mud too,
but he didn't cry.
And neither did Ma.

March 1934

Spring 1934

Tested by Dust

While we sat
taking our six-weeks test,
the wind rose
and the sand blew
right through the cracks
    in the schoolhouse wall,
right through the gaps
    around the window glass,
and by the time the tests were done,
each and every one of us
was coughing pretty good and we all
needed a bath.

I hope we get bonus points
for testing in a dust storm.

April 1934

Banks

Ma says,
everything we lost
when the banks closed
'cause they didn't have enough cash
  to go around,
all the money that's ours
is coming back to us in full.

Good.

Now we have money for a doctor
when the baby comes.

April 1934

Beat Wheat

County Agent Dewey
had some pretty bad news.
One quarter of the wheat is lost:
blown away or withered up.
What remains is little more than
a wisp of what it should be.
And every day we have no rain,
more wheat dies.

County Agent Dewey says, "Soon
there won't be enough wheat
for seed to plant next fall."

The piano is some comfort in all this.
I go to it and I forget the dust for hours,
testing my long fingers on wild rhythms,
but Ma slams around in the kitchen
    when I play
and after a while she sends me to the store.
Joe De La Flor doesn't see me pass him by;
he rides his fences, dazed by dust.
I wince at the sight of his rib-thin cattle.
But he's not even seeing them.
I look at Joe and know our future
    is drying up
and blowing away with the dust.

April 1934

Give Up on Wheat

Ma says,
"Try putting in a pond, Bayard.
We can fill it off the windmill.
We've got a good well."

Daddy grumbles, "The water'll seep
back into the ground
as fast as I can pump it, Pol.
We'll dry up our well
and then we'll have nothing."

"Plant some other things, then," Ma says.
"Try cotton,
sorghum. If we plant the fields
   in different crops,
maybe some will do better,
better than wheat."

Daddy says,
"No.
It has to be wheat.
I've grown it before.
I'll grow it again."

But Ma says, "Can't you see
what's happening, Bayard?
The wheat's not meant to be here."

And Daddy says,
"What about those apple trees of yours, Pol?
You think they are?
Nothing needs more to drink
  than those two.
But you wouldn't hear
  of leveling your apples,
would you?"

Ma is bittering. I can see it in her mouth.
"A pond would work," she says,
sounding crusty and stubborn.

And Daddy says, "Look it, Pol,
  who's the farmer?
You or me?"

Ma says,
"Who pays the bills?"

"No one right now," Daddy says.

Ma starts to quaking
  but she won't let Daddy see.
Instead, she goes out to the chickens
and
her anger,
simmering over like a pot
  in an empty kitchen,
boils itself down doing chores.

April 1934

What I Don't Know

My teacher, Miss Freeland,
is singing
at the Shrine
along with famous
opera stars
from all around the country
in a play called
Madame Butterfly.

I've never heard of that play.

"Most everyone's heard of
  Madame Butterfly,"
Mad Dog says.

How does that
singing plowboy know something I don't?
And how much more is out there
most everyone else has heard of
except me?

April 1934

Apple Blossoms

Ma
has been nursing these two trees
for as long as I can remember.
In spite of the dust,
in spite of the drought,
because of Ma's stubborn care,
these trees are
thick with blossoms,
delicate and
pinky-white.

My eyes can't get enough of the sight
    of them.
I stand under the trees
and let the petals
fall into my hair,
a blizzard
of sweet-smelling flowers,
dropped from the boughs of the two
placed there
in the front yard by Ma
before I was born,
that she and they might bring forth fruit
into our home,
together.

May 1934

World War

Daddy was just seventeen
when he fought in the
Great War off in France.

There's not much he's willing to
say about those days,
   except about the poppies.
He remembers the poppies,
red on the graves of the dead.

Daddy says
that war tore France up
worse than a tornado,
worse than a dust storm,
but no matter,
the wild poppies bloomed in the trail
   of the fighting,
brightening the French countryside.

I wish I could see poppies
growing out of this dust.

May 1934

Apples

Ma's apple blossoms
have turned to hard green balls.

To eat them now,
so tart,
would turn my mouth inside out,
would make my stomach groan.

But in just a couple months,
after the baby is born,
those apples will be ready
and we'll make pies
and sauce
and pudding
and dumplings
and cake
and cobbler
and have just plain apples to take to school
and slice with my pocket knife
and eat one juicy piece at a time
until my mouth is clean
and fresh
and my breath is nothing but apple.

June 1934

Dust and Rain

On Sunday,
winds came,
bringing a red dust
like prairie fire,
hot and peppery,
searing the inside of my nose,
the whites of my eyes.
Roaring dust,
turning the day from sunlight to midnight.

And as the dust left,
rain came.
Rain that was no blessing.
It came too hard,
too fast,
and washed the soil away,
washed the wheat away with it.
Now
little remains of Daddy's hard work.
And the only choice he has
is to give up or
start all over again.

At the Strong ranch
they didn't get a single drop.
So who fared better?

Ma looks out the window at her apple trees.
Hard green balls have dropped
   to the ground.
But there are enough left;
enough
for a small harvest,
if we lose no more.

June 1934

Harvest

The combines have started moving
  across the fields,
bringing in wheat,
whatever has managed to grow.

Mr. Tuttle delivered the first load to town
selling it for seventy-three cents a bushel.
Not bad.

Mr. Chaffin, Mr. Haverstick,
  and Mr. French,
they've delivered their harvest too,
dropping it at the Joyce City grain elevator.

Daddy asked Mr. Haverstick
  how things looked
and Mr. Haverstick said he figures
he took eight bushels
  off a twenty-bushel acre.

If Daddy gets five bushels to his acre
it'll be a miracle.

June 1934

On the Road with Arley

Here's the way I figure it.
My place in the world is at the piano.
I'm earning a little money playing,
thanks to Arley Wanderdale.
He and his Black Mesa Boys
    have connections in
Keyes and Goodwell and Texhoma.
And every little crowd
is grateful to hear a rag or two played
on the piano
by a long-legged, red-haired girl,
even when the piano has a few keys
    soured by dust.

At first Ma crossed her arms
against her chest
and stared me down,
hard-jawed and sharp,
    and said I couldn't go.
But the money helped convince her,
and the compliment from Arley
    and his wife, Vera,
that they'd surely bring my ma along
    to play too,
if she wasn't so far gone with a baby coming.
Ma said

okay,
but only for the summer,
and only if she didn't hear me gripe
    how I was tired,
or see me dragging my back end around,
or have to call me twice upon a morning,
or find my farm chores falling down,
and only if Arley's wife, Vera,
    kept an eye on me.

Arley says my piano playing is good.
I play a set of songs with the word *baby*
    in the title,
like "My Baby Just Cares for Me"
and "Walking My Baby Back Home."
I picked those songs on purpose for Ma,
and the folks that come to hear Arley's band,
they like them fine.

Arley pays in dimes.
Ma's putting my earnings away
    I don't know where,
saving it to send me to school in a few years.
The money doesn't matter much to me.
I'd play for nothing.
When I'm with Arley's boys
    we forget the dust.
We are flying down the road in Arley's car,
singing,
laying our voices on top of the

beat Miller Rice plays on the back
   of Arley's seat,
and sometimes, Vera, up front,
   chirps crazy notes with
no words
and the sounds she makes
   seem just about amazing.

It's being part of all that,
being part of Arley's crowd I like so much,
being on the road,
being somewhere new and interesting.
We have a fine time.

And they let me play piano, too.

June 1934

Summer 1934

Hope in a Drizzle

Quarter inch of rain
is nothing to complain about.
It'll help the plants above ground,
and start the new seeds growing.

That quarter inch of rain
   did wonders for Ma, too,
who is ripe as a melon these days.
She has nothing to say to anyone anymore,
except how she aches for rain,
at breakfast,
at dinner,
all day,
all night,
she aches for rain.

Today, she stood out in the drizzle
hidden from the road,
and from Daddy,
and she thought from me,
but I could see her from the barn,
she was bare as a pear,
raindrops
sliding down her skin,
leaving traces of mud on her face
   and her long back,

trickling dark and light paths,
slow tracks of wet dust
   down the bulge of her belly.
My dazzling ma, round and ripe and striped
like a melon.

July 1934

Dionne Quintuplets

While the dust blew
down our road,
against our house,
across our fields,
up in Canada
a lady named Elzire Dionne
gave birth to five baby girls
all at once.

I looked at Ma,
so pregnant with one baby.
"Can you imagine five?" I said.
Ma lowered herself into a chair.
Tears dropping on her tight stretched belly,
she wept
just to think of it.

July 1934

Wild Boy of the Road

A boy came by the house today,
he asked for food.
He couldn't pay anything,
   but Ma set him down
and gave him biscuits
and milk.
He offered to work for his meal,
Ma sent him out to see Daddy.
The boy and Daddy came back late
   in the afternoon.
The boy walked two steps behind,
in Daddy's dust.
He wasn't more than sixteen.
Thin as a fence rail.
I wondered what
Livie Killian's brother looked like now.
I wondered about Livie herself.
Daddy asked if the boy wanted a bath,
a haircut,
a change of clothes before he moved on.
The boy nodded.
I never heard him say more than "Yes, sir" or
"No, sir" or
"Much obliged."

We watched him walk away

down the road,
in a pair of Daddy's mended overalls,
his legs like willow limbs,
his arms like reeds.
Ma rested her hands on her heavy stomach,
Daddy rested his chin
  on the top of my head.
"His mother is worrying about him,"
  Ma said.
"His mother is wishing her boy
  would come home."

Lots of mothers wishing that these days,
while their sons walk to California,
where rain comes,
and the color green doesn't seem
  like such a miracle,
and hope rises daily, like sap in a stem.
And I think, some day I'm going
  to walk there too,
through New Mexico and Arizona
  and Nevada.
Some day I'll leave behind the wind,
  and the dust
and walk my way West
and make myself to home
  in that distant place
of green vines and promise.

July 1934

The Accident

I got
burned
bad.

Daddy
put a pail of kerosene
next to the stove
and Ma,
fixing breakfast,
thinking the pail was
filled with water,
lifted it,
to make Daddy's coffee,
poured it,
but instead of making coffee,
Ma made a rope of fire.
It rose up from the stove
to the pail
and the kerosene burst
into flames.

Ma ran across the kitchen,
out the porch door,
screaming for Daddy.
I tore after her,
then,

thinking of the burning pail
left behind in the bone-dry kitchen,
I flew back and grabbed it,
throwing it out the door.

I didn't know.
I didn't know Ma was coming back.

The flaming oil
splashed
onto her apron,
and Ma,
suddenly Ma,
was a column of fire.
I pushed her to the ground,
desperate to save her,
desperate to save the baby, I
tried,
beating out the flames with my hands.
I did the best I could.
But it was no good.
Ma
got
burned
bad.

July 1934

Burns

At first I felt no pain,
only heat.

I thought I might be swallowed by the heat,
like the witch in "Hansel and Gretel,"
and nothing would be left of me.

Someone brought Doc Rice.
He tended Ma first,
then came to me.
The doctor cut away the skin on my hands,
    it hung in
crested strips.
He cut my skin away with scissors,
then poked my hands with pins
    to see what I could
feel.
He bathed my burns in antiseptic.

Only then the pain came.

July 1934

Nightmare

I am awake now,
still shaking from my dream:

I was coming home
through a howling dust storm,
my lowered face was scrubbed raw
    by dirt and wind.
Grit scratched my eyes,
it crunched between my teeth.
Sand chafed inside my clothes,
against my skin.
Dust crept inside my ears, up my nose,
down my throat.
I shuddered, nasty with dust.

In the house,
dust blew through the cracks in the walls,
it covered the floorboards and
heaped against the doors.
It floated in the air, everywhere.
I didn't care about anyone, anything,
    only the piano. I
searched for it,
found it under a mound of dust.
I was angry at Ma for letting in the dust.
I cleaned off the keys

but when I played,
a tortured sound came from the piano,
like someone shrieking.
I hit the keys with my fist,
    and the piano broke into
a hundred pieces.

Daddy called to me. He asked me
    to bring water,
Ma was thirsty.
I brought up a pail of fire
    and Ma drank it. She had
given birth to a baby of flames. The baby
burned at her side.

I ran away. To the Eatons' farm.
The house had been tractored out,
tipped off its foundation.
No one could live there.
Everywhere I looked were dunes
    of rippled dust.
The wind roared like fire.
The door to the house hung open
    and there was
dust inside
several feet deep.
And there was a piano.

The bench was gone, right through the floor.
The piano leaned toward me.

I stood and played.
The relief I felt to hear the sound of music
    after the
sound
of the piano at home. . . .

I dragged the Eatons' piano
    through the dust
to our house,
but when I got it there I couldn't play.
    I had swollen
lumps for hands,
they dripped a sickly pus,
they swung stupidly from my wrists,
they stung with pain.

When I woke up, the part
about my hands
was real.

July 1934

A Tent of Pain

Daddy
has made a tent out of the sheet over Ma
so nothing will touch her skin,
what skin she has left.
I can't look at her,
I can't recognize her.
She smells like scorched meat.
Her body groaning there,
it looks nothing like my ma.
It doesn't even have a face.

Daddy brings her water,
and drips it inside the slit of her mouth
by squeezing a cloth.
She can't open her eyes,
she cries out
when the baby moves inside her,
otherwise she moans,
day and night.
I wish the dust would plug my ears
so I couldn't hear her.

July 1934

Drinking

Daddy found the money
Ma kept squirreled in the kitchen
  under the
threshold.

It wasn't very much.
But it was enough for him
  to get good and drunk.

He went out last night.
While Ma moaned and begged for water.
He drank up the emergency money
until it was gone.

I tried to help her.
I couldn't aim the dripping cloth
  into her mouth.
I couldn't squeeze.
It hurt the blisters on my hands to try.
I only made it worse for Ma. She cried
for the pain of the water running
  into her sores,
she cried for the water that
would not soothe her throat
and quench her thirst,
and the whole time
my father was in Guymon,
drinking.

July 1934

Devoured

Doc sent me outside to get water.
The day was so hot,
the house was so hot.
As I came out the door,
I saw the cloud descending.
It whirred like a thousand engines.
It shifted shape as it came
settling first over Daddy's wheat.
Grasshoppers,
eating tassles, leaves, stalks.
Then coming closer to the house,
eating Ma's garden, the fence posts,
the laundry on the line, and then,
the grasshoppers came right over me,
descending on Ma's apple trees.
I climbed into the trees,
opening scabs on my tender hands,
grasshoppers clinging to me.
I tried beating them away.
But the grasshoppers ate every leaf,
they ate every piece of fruit.
Nothing left but a couple apple cores,
hanging from Ma's trees.
I couldn't tell her,
couldn't bring myself to say
her apples were gone.

I never had a chance.

Ma died that day
giving birth to my brother.

August 1934

Blame

My father's sister came to fetch my brother,
even as Ma's body cooled.
She came to bring my brother back
    to Lubbock
to raise as her own,
but my brother died before Aunt Ellis
    got here.
She wouldn't even hold his little body.
She barely noticed me.
As soon as she found my brother dead,
she
had a talk with my father.
Then she turned around
and headed back to Lubbock.

The neighbor women came.
They wrapped my baby brother in a blanket
and placed him in Ma's bandaged arms.
We buried them together
on the rise Ma loved,
the one she gazed at
    from the kitchen window,
the one that looks out over the
dried-up Beaver River.

Reverend Bingham led the service.
He talked about Ma,
but what he said made no sense
and I could tell

he didn't truly know her,
he'd never even heard her play piano.
He asked my father
to name my baby brother.
My father, hunched over, said nothing.
I spoke up in my father's silence.
I told the reverend
my brother's name was Franklin.
Like our President.

The women talked as they
scrubbed death from our house.
I
stayed in my room
silent on the iron bed,
listening to their voices.

"Billie Jo threw the pail,"
they said. "An accident,"
they said.
Under their words a finger pointed.

They didn't talk
about my father leaving kerosene
    by the stove.
They didn't say a word about my father
drinking himself
into a stupor
while Ma writhed, begging for water.
They only said,
Billie Jo threw the pail of kerosene.

August 1934

Birthday

I walk to town.
I don't look back over my shoulder
at the single grave
holding Ma and my little brother.
I am trying not to look back at anything.

Dust rises with each step,
there's a greasy smell to the air.
On either side of the road are
the carcasses of jackrabbits, small birds,
   field mice,
stretching out into the distance.

My father stares out across his land,
empty but for a few withered stalks
like the tufts on an old man's head.
I don't know if he thinks more of Ma,
or the wheat that used to grow here.

There is barely a blade of grass
swaying in the stinging wind,
there are only these
lumps of flesh
that once were hands long enough
   to span octaves,
swinging at my sides.

I come up quiet
and sit behind Arley Wanderdale's house,
where no one can see me,
    and lean my head back,
and close my eyes,
and listen to Arley play.

August 1934

Roots

President Roosevelt tells us to
plant trees. Trees will
break the wind. He says,
trees
will end the drought,
the animals can take shelter there,
children can take shelter.
Trees have roots, he says.
They hold on to the land.

That's good advice, but
I'm not sure he understands the problem.

Trees have never been at home here.
They're just not meant to be here.
Maybe none of us are meant to be here,
only the prairie grass
and the hawks.

My father will stay, no matter what,
he's stubborn as sod.
He and the land have a hold on each other.
But what about me?

August 1934

The Empty Spaces

I don't know my father anymore.
He sits across from me,
he looks like my father,
he chews his food like my father,
he brushes his dusty hair back
like my father,
but he is a stranger.

I am awkward with him,
and irritated,
and I want to be alone
but I am terrified of being alone.

We are both changing,
we are shifting to fill in the empty spaces
    left by Ma.
I keep my raw and stinging hands
behind my back when he comes near
because he
stares
when he sees them.

September 1934

The Hole

The heat from the cookstove
    hurts my burns,
and the salt,
the water, and the dust hurt too.
I spend all my time in pain,
and
my father spends his time out the side
    of the house,
digging a hole,
forty feet by sixty feet,
six feet deep.

I think he is digging the pond,
to feed off the windmill,
the one Ma wanted,
but he doesn't say. He just digs.

He sends me to the train yard
    to gather boards,
boards that once were box cars
but now are junk.
I bring them back,
    careful of the scabs and the
raw sores on my bare hands.
I don't know what he needs boards for.
He doesn't tell me.

When he's not in the hole, digging,
he works on the windmill,
replacing the parts
that kept it from turning.

People stop by and watch.
  They think my father is
crazy
digging such a big hole.
I think he's crazy too.
The water will seep back into the earth.
It'll never stay put in any old pond.
But my father has thought through all that
and he's digging anyway.

I think to talk to Ma about it,
and then I remember.

I can almost forgive him the taking
  of Ma's money,
I can almost forgive him
  his night in Guymon,
getting drunk.
But as long as I live,
no matter how big a hole he digs,
I can't forgive him that pail of kerosene
left by the side of the stove.

September 1934

Kilauea

A volcano erupted in Hawaii.
Kilauea.
It threw huge
chunks
into the air,
the ground shook,
and smoke
choked everything in its path.

. . . sounds a little
like a dust storm.

September 1934

Boxes

In my closet are two boxes,
the gatherings of my life,
papers,
school drawings,
a broken hairpin,
a dress from my baby days,
my first lock of hair,
a tiny basket woven from prairie grass,
a doll with a china head,
a pink ball,
three dozen marbles,
a fan from Baxter's Funeral Home,
my baby teeth in a glass jar,
a torn map of the world,
two candy wrappers,
a thousand things I haven't looked at
in years.
I kept promising to go through the boxes
with Ma
and get rid of what I didn't need,
but I never got to it
and now my hands hurt.
And I haven't got the heart.

September 1934

Night Bloomer

Mrs. Brown's
cereus plant bloomed on Saturday night.
She sent word
after promising I could come see it.
I rubbed my gritty eyes with swollen hands.
My stomach grizzled as I
made my way through the dark
to her house.
Ma wouldn't have let me go at all.
My father just stood in the doorway and
watched me leave.

It was almost three in the morning
    when I got there.
A small crowd stood around.
Mrs. Brown said,
"The blossom opened at midnight,
big as a dinner plate.
It took only moments to unfold."

How can such a flower
find a way to bloom in this drought,
in this wind.

It blossomed at night,
when the sun couldn't scorch it,

when the wind was quiet,
when there might have been a sip of dew
to freshen it.

I couldn't watch at dawn,
when the flower,
touched by the first finger of morning light,
wilted and died.
I couldn't watch
as the tender petals burned up in the sun.

September 1934

The Path of Our Sorrow

Miss Freeland said,
"During the Great War we fed the world.
We couldn't grow enough wheat
to fill all the bellies.
The price the world paid for our wheat
was so high
it swelled our wallets
and our heads,
and we bought bigger tractors,
more acres,
until we had mortgages
and rent
and bills
beyond reason,
but we all felt so useful, we didn't notice.
Then the war ended and before long,
Europe didn't need our wheat anymore,
they could grow their own.
But we needed Europe's money
to pay our mortgage,
our rent,
our bills.
We squeezed more cattle,
more sheep,
onto less land,
and they grazed down the stubble

till they reached root.
And the price of wheat kept dropping
so we had to grow more bushels
to make the same amount
    of money we made before,
to pay for all that equipment, all that land,
and the more sod we plowed up,
the drier things got,
because the water that used to collect there
under the grass,
biding its time,
keeping things alive through the dry spells
wasn't there anymore.
Without the sod the water vanished,
the soil turned to dust.
Until the wind took it,
lifting it up and carrying it away.
Such a sorrow doesn't come suddenly,
there are a thousand steps to take
before you get there."
But now,
sorrow climbs up our front steps,
big as Texas,
    and we didn't even see it coming,
even though it'd been making
    its way straight for us
all along.

September 1934

Autumn 1934

Hired Work

My father hired on
at Wireless Power on Tuesday,
excavating for towers.

He said,
"I'm good at digging,"
and everyone who knows about our hole
knows he's telling the truth.

He might as well earn a couple dollars.
It doesn't look good for the winter crop.
Earning some cash will make him feel better.
I don't think he'll drink it up.
He hasn't done that since Ma

It's hard to believe
   I once brought money in too,
even if it was just a dime now and then,
for playing piano.
Now I can't hardly stay
   in the same room with one.
Especially Ma's.

October 1934

Almost Rain

It almost rained Saturday.
The clouds hung low over the farm.
The air felt thick.
It smelled like rain.

In town,
the sidewalks
got damp.
That was all.

November 1934

Those Hands

The Wildcats started practice this week.
Coach Albright used to say I could play
   for the team.
"You've got what it takes, Billie Jo.
Look at the size of those hands,"
   he'd say. "Look at
how tall."
I'd tell him, "Just because I'm tall
   doesn't mean I can
play basketball,
or even that I want to."
But he'd say I should play anyway.

Coach Albright didn't say anything
   to me about
basketball this year.
I haven't gotten any shorter.
It's because of my hands.

My father used to say,
   why not put those hands to
good use?
He doesn't say anything
   about "those hands"
anymore.
Only Arley Wanderdale talks about them,
and how they could play piano again,
if I would only try.

November 1934

Real Snow

The dust stopped,
and it
snowed.
Real snow.
Dreamy Christmas snow,
gentle,
nothing blowing,
such calm,
like after a fever,
wet,
clinging to the earth,
melting into the dirt,
snow.

Oh, the grass, and the wheat
and the cattle,
and the rabbits,
and my father will be happy.

November 1934

Dance Revue

Vera Wanderdale
is putting on a dance revue
  at the Palace
and Arley asked
if I'd play a number
  with the Black Mesa Boys.
It's hard, coming on to Christmas,
just me and my father,
with no Ma and no little brother.
I don't really feel like doing anything.
Still, I told Arley I would try,
just because it looked like it meant
  a lot to him.
He said he'd be dancing then,
so he needed a piano player,
and Mad Dog would be singing,
and he knew how I'd just love to be
connected with anything Mad Dog's doing.

The costumes Vera ordered
come all the way from the city, she said.
Special,
the latest cuts.
I wish I could go with her
to pick them up.

During rehearsals,
Mad Dog comes off the stage
   after his numbers
and stands by the piano.
He doesn't look at me like
I'm a poor motherless thing.
He doesn't stare at my deformed hands.
He looks at me like I am
someone he knows,
someone named Billie Jo Kelby.
I'm grateful for that,
especially considering how bad I'm playing.

December 1934

Mad Dog's Tale

Mad Dog is surrounded by girls.
They ask him how he got his name.
He says, "It's not because I'm wild,
or a crazy, untamed boy,
but because fourteen years ago
    when I was two
I would bite anything I could catch hold of:
    my ma,
my brother, Doc Rice,
    even Reverend Bingham.
So my father named me Mad Dog.
And it stuck."

When I go home
I ask my father if he knows Mad Dog's
real name.
He looks at me like I'm talking
    in another language.

Ma could have told me.

December 1934

Art Exhibit

We had an art exhibit last week
in the basement of the courthouse,
to benefit the library.
Price of admission was one book
or ten cents.
I paid ten cents the first time,
but they let me in the second
   and third times for free.
That was awful kind,
since I didn't have another dime
and I couldn't bring myself to
hand over Ma's book of poetry
from the shelf over the piano.

It was really something
   to see the oil paintings,
the watercolors,
the pastels and charcoals.
There were pictures of the Panhandle
   in the old days
with the grass blowing and wolves,
there was a painting of a woman
   getting dressed
in a room of curtains,
and a drawing of a railroad station
with a garden out the front,

and a sketch of a little girl
  holding an enormous cat
in her lap.

But now the exhibit is gone,
the paintings
stored away in spare rooms
or locked up
where no one can see them.
I feel such a hunger
to see such things.
And such an anger
because I can't.

December 1934

Winter 1935

State Tests Again

Miss Freeland said
our grade
topped the entire state of Oklahoma
on the state tests again, twenty-four
points higher
than the state average.

Wish I could run home and tell Ma
and see her nod
and hear her say,

"I knew you could."

It would be enough.

January 1935

Christmas Dinner
Without the Cranberry Sauce

Miss Freeland
was my ma
at the school
Christmas dinner.

I thought I'd be
the only one
without a
real ma,
but two other motherless girls came.

We served turkey,
chestnut dressing,
sweet potatoes, and brown gravy.
Made it all ourselves
and it came out
pretty good,
better than the Christmas dinner
　　I made for my
father
at home,
where we sat at the table,
silent, just the two of us.

Being there without Ma,
without the baby,
wouldn't have been so bad,
if I'd just remembered the cranberry sauce.
My father loved Ma's
    special cranberry sauce.
But she never showed me how to make it.

January 1935

Driving the Cows

Dust
piles up like snow
across the prairie,
dunes leaning against fences,
mountains of dust pushing over barns.
Joe De La Flor can't afford to feed his cows,
can't afford to sell them.
County Agent Dewey comes,
takes the cows behind the barn,
and shoots them.
Too hard to
watch their lungs clog with dust,
like our chickens, suffocated.
Better to let the government take them,
than suffer the sight of their bony hides
sinking down
into the earth.

Joe De La Flor
rides the range.
Come spring he'll gather Russian thistle,
pulling the plant while it's still green
    and young,
before the prickles form, before it breaks free
to tumble across the plains.
He gathers thistle to feed

what's left of his cattle,
his bone-thin cattle,
cattle he drives away
from the dried-up Beaver River,
to where the Cimarron still runs,
pushing the herd across the breaks,
where they might last another week,
maybe two,
until it
rains.

January 1935

First Rain

Sunday night,
I stretch my legs in my iron bed
under the roof.
I place a wet cloth over my nose to keep
from breathing dust
and wipe the grime tracings
   from around my mouth,
and shiver, thinking of Ma.
I am kept company by the sound of my heart
drumming.

Restless,
I tangle in the dusty sheets,
sending the sand flying,
cursing the grit against my skin,
between my teeth,
under my lids,
swearing I'll leave this forsaken place.

I hear the first drops.
Like the tapping of a stranger
at the door of a dream,
the rain changes everything.
It strokes the roof,
streaking the dusty tin,
ponging,

a concert of rain notes,
spilling from gutters,
gushing through gullies,
soaking into the thirsty earth outside.

Monday morning dawns,
cloaked in mist.
I button into my dress, slip on my sweater,
and push my way off the porch,
sticking my face into the fog,
into the moist skin of the fog.
The sound of dripping surrounds me as I
walk to town.

Soaked to my underwear,
I can't bear to go
through the schoolhouse door,
I want only to stand in the rain.

Monday afternoon,
Joe De La Flor brushes mud from his horse,
Mr. Kincannon hires my father
to pull his Olds out of the muck
    on Route 64.

And later,
when the clouds lift,
the farmers, surveying their fields,
nod their heads as
the frail stalks revive,

everyone, everything, grateful
    for this moment,
free of the
weight of dust.

January 1935

Haydon P. Nye

Haydon P. Nye died this week.
I knew him to wave,
he liked the way I played piano.

The newspaper said
    when Haydon first came
he could see only grass,
grass and wild horses and wolves roaming.

Then folks moved in and sod got busted
and bushels of wheat turned the plains
    to gold,
and Haydon P. Nye
grabbed the Oklahoma Panhandle in his fist
and held on.

By the time the railroad came in
on land Haydon sold them,
the buffalo and the wild horses had gone.

Some years
Haydon Nye saw the sun dry up his crop,
saw the grasshoppers chew it down,
but then came years of rain
and the wheat thrived,
and his pockets filled,

and his big laugh came easy.

They buried Haydon Nye on his land,
busted more sod to lay down his bones.
Will they sow wheat on his grave,
where the buffalo
once grazed?

January 1935

Scrubbing Up Dust

Walking past the Crystal Hotel
I saw Jim Martin down on his knees.
He was scraping up mud that had
dried to crust
after the rain mixed with dust Sunday last.

When I got home
I took a good look at the steps
and the porch
and the windows.
I saw them with Ma's eyes
   and thought about
how she'd been haunting me.

I thought about Ma,
who would've washed clothes,
beaten furniture,
aired rugs,
scrubbed floors,
down on her knees,
brush in hand,
breaking that mud
like the farmers break sod,
always watching over her shoulder
for the next duster to roll in.

My stubborn ma,
she'd be doing it all
with my brother Franklin to tend to.
She never could stand a mess.
My father doesn't notice the dried mud.
Least he never tells me,
not that he tells me much of anything
    these days.
With Ma gone,
if the mud's to be busted,
the job falls to me.
It isn't the work I hate,
the knuckle-breaking work
    of beating mud out of
every blessed thing,
but every day
my fingers and hands
ache so bad. I think
I should just let them rest,
let the dust rest,
let the world rest.
But I can't leave it rest,
on account of Ma,
haunting.

January 1935

Outlined by Dust

My father stares at me
while I sit across from him at the table,
while I wash dishes in the basin,
my back to him,
the picked and festered bits
    of my hands in agony.
He stares at me
as I empty the wash water at the roots
of Ma's apple trees.

He spends long days
digging for the electric-train folks
when they can use him,
or working here,
nursing along the wheat,
what there is of it,
or digging the pond.

He sings sometimes under his breath,
even now,
even after so much sorrow.
He sings a man's song,
deep with what has happened to us.
It doesn't swing lightly
the way Ma's voice did,
the way Miss Freeland's voice does,

the way Mad Dog sings.
My father's voice starts and stops,
like a car short of gas,
like an engine choked with dust,
but then he clears his throat
and the song starts up again.

He rubs his eyes
the way I do,
with his palms out.
Ma never did that.
And he wipes the milk from his
upper lip same as me,
with his thumb and forefinger.
Ma never did that, either.

We don't talk much.
My father never was a talker.
Ma's dying hasn't changed that.
I guess he gets the sound out of him with the
songs he sings.

I can't help thinking
how it is for him,
without Ma.
Waking up alone, only
his shape
left in the bed,
outlined by dust.
He always smelled a little like her

first thing in the morning,
when he left her in bed
and went out to do the milking.
She'd scuff into the kitchen
    a few minutes later,
bleary eyed,
to start breakfast.
I don't think she was ever
really meant for farm life,
I think once she had bigger dreams,
but she made herself over
to fit my father.

Now he smells of dust
and coffee,
tobacco and cows.
None of the musky woman smell left
    that was Ma.

He stares at me,
maybe he is looking for Ma.
He won't find her.
I look like him,
I stand like him,
I walk across the kitchen floor
with that long-legged walk
of his.
I can't make myself over the way Ma did.
And yet, if I could look in the mirror
    and see her in

my face.
If I could somehow know that Ma
and baby Franklin
lived on in me . . .

But it can't be.
I'm my father's daughter.

January 1935

The President's Ball

All across the land,
couples dancing,
arm in arm, hand in hand,
at the Birthday Ball.

My father puts on his best overalls,
I wear my Sunday dress,
the one with the white collar,
and we walk to town
to the Legion Hall
and join the dance. Our feet flying,
me and my father,
on the wooden floor whirling
to Arley Wanderdale
    and the Black Mesa Boys.

Till ten,
when Arley stands up from the piano,
to announce we raised thirty-three dollars
for infantile paralysis,
a little better than last year.

And I remember last year,
when Ma was alive and we were
crazy excited about the baby coming.
And I played at this same party

for Franklin D.
Roosevelt
and Joyce City
and Arley.

Tonight, for a little while
in the bright hall folks were almost free,
almost free of dust,
almost free of debt,
almost free of fields of withered wheat.
Most of the night I think I smiled.
And twice my father laughed.
Imagine.

January 1935

Lunch

No one's going hungry at school today.
The government
sent canned meat,
rice,
potatoes.
The bakery
sent loaves of bread,
and
Scotty Moore, George Nall,
    and Willie Harkins
brought in milk,
fresh creamy milk
straight from their farms.
Real lunch and then
stomachs
full and feeling fine
for classes
in the afternoon.

The little ones drank themselves
    into white
mustaches,
they ate
and ate,
until pushing back from their desks,
their stomachs round,

they swore they'd never eat again.
The older girls,
Elizabeth and LoRaine,
    helped Miss Freeland
cook,
and Hillary and I,
we served and washed,
our ears ringing with the sound
    of satisfied children.

February 1935

Guests

In our classroom this morning,
we came in to find a family no one knew.

They were shy,
a little frightened,
embarrassed.
A man and his wife, pretty far along
    with a baby
coming,

a baby
coming

two little kids
and a grandma.
They'd moved into our classroom
    during the night.
An iron bed
and some pasteboard boxes.
    That's all they had.
They'd cleaned the room first,
    and arranged it,
making a private place for themselves.

"I'm on the look for a job," the man said.
"The dust blew so mean last night

I thought to shelter my family here awhile."

The two little kids turned their big eyes
from Miss Freeland
back to their father.

"I can't have my wife sleeping
in the cold truck,
not now. Not with the baby coming
so soon."

Miss Freeland said they could stay
as long as they wanted.

February 1935

Family School

Every day we bring fixings for soup
and put a big pot on to simmer.
We share it at lunch with our guests,
the family of migrants who have moved out
   from dust
and Depression
and moved into our classroom.
We are careful to take only so much to eat,
making sure there's enough soup
   left in the pot for
their supper.

Some of us bring in toys
and clothes for the children.
I found a few things of my brother's
and brought them to school,
little feed-sack nighties,
so small,
so full of hope.

Franklin
never wore a one of the nighties
   Ma made him,
except the one we buried him in.

The man, Buddy Williams,
helps out around the school,
fixing windows and doors,
and the bad spot on the steps,
cleaning up the school yard
so it never looked so good.

The grandma takes care of the children,
bringing them out
    when the dust isn't blowing,
letting them chase tumbleweeds
    across the field
behind the school,
but when the dust blows,
the family sits in their little apartment
    inside our
classroom,
studying Miss Freeland's lessons
right alongside us.

February 1935

Birth

One morning when I arrive at school
Miss Freeland says to keep the kids out,
that the baby is coming
and no one can enter the building
until the birthing is done.
I think about Ma
and how that birth went.
I keep the kids out and listen behind me,
praying for the sound of a baby
crying into this world,
and not the silence
my brother brought with him.
And then the cry comes
and I have to go away for a little while
and just walk off the feelings.

Miss Freeland rings the bell to call us in
but I'm not ready to come back yet.
When I do come,
I study how fine that baby girl is.
   How perfect,
and that she is wearing
   a feed-sack nightgown that
was my brother's.

February 1935

Time to Go

They left a couple weeks
   after the baby came,
all of them crammed inside
   that rusty old truck.
I ran half a mile in their dust to catch them.
I didn't want to let that baby go.
"Wait for me," I cried,
choking on the cloud that rose behind them.
But they didn't hear me.
They were heading west.
And no one was looking back.

February 1935

Something Sweet from Moonshine

Ashby Durwin
and his pal Rush
had themselves a
fine operation on the Cimarron River,
where the water still runs a little,
though the fish are mostly dead
from the dust floating on the surface.
Ashby and Rush
    were cooking up moonshine
in their giant metal still on the bank
when Sheriff Robertson caught them.
He found jugs of finished whiskey,
and barrels and barrels of mash,
he found two sacks of rye,
and he found sugar,
one thousand pounds of sugar.

The government men
    took Ashby and Rush off to
Enid
for breaking the law,
but Sheriff Robertson stayed behind,
took apart the still,
washed away the whiskey and the mash,
and thought about that sugar,
all that sugar, one-half ton of sugar.

Sheriff decided
some should find its way
into the mouths of us kids.
Bake for them, Miss Freeland, he said,
bake them cakes and cookies and pies,
cook them custard and cobbler and crisp,
make them candy and taffy
    and apple pandowdy.

Apple pandowdy!

These kids,
Sheriff Robertson said,
ought to have something sweet to
wash down their dusty milk.
And so we did.

February 1935

Dreams

Each day after class lets out,
each morning before it begins,
I sit at the school piano
and make my hands work.
In spite of the pain,
in spite of the stiffness
and scars.
I make my hands play piano.
I have practiced my best piece over and over
till my arms throb,
because Thursday night
the Palace Theatre is having a contest.
Any man, woman, or child
who sings,
dances,
reads,
or plays worth a lick
can climb onto that stage.
Just register by four p.m.
and give them a taste of what you can do
and you're in,
performing for the crowd,
warming up the audience for the
Hazel Hurd Players.
I figure if I practice enough
I won't shame myself.

And we sure could use the extra cash
if I won.
Three-dollar first prize,
two-dollar second,
one-dollar third.
But I don't know if I could win anything,
not anymore.
It's the playing I want most,
the proving I can still do it.
Without Arley making excuses.
I have a hunger,
for more than food.
I have a hunger
bigger than Joyce City.
I want tongues to tie, and
eyes to shine at me
like they do at Mad Dog Craddock.
Course they never will,
not with my hands all scarred up,
looking like the earth itself,
all parched and rough and cracking,
but if I played right enough,
maybe they would see past my hands.
Maybe they could feel at ease with me again,
and maybe then,
I could feel at ease with myself.

February 1935

The Competition

I suppose everyone in Joyce City
   and beyond,
all the way to Felt
and Keyes
and even Guymon,
came to watch the talent show at the Palace,
Thursday night.

Backstage,
we were seventeen amateur acts,
our wild hearts pounding,
our lips sticking to our teeth,
our urge to empty ourselves
top and bottom,
made a sorry sight
in front of the
famous Hazel Hurd Players.

But they were kind to us,
helped us with our makeup and our hair,
showed us where to stand,
how to bow,
and the quickest route to the
toilet.

The audience hummed

on the other side of the
closed curtain,
Ivy Huxford
kept peeking out and giving reports
of who was there,
and how she never saw so many seats
filled in the Palace,
and that she didn't think they could
squeeze a
rattlesnake
into the back
even if he paid full price,
the place was so packed.

My father told me he'd come
once chores were done.
I guess he did.

The Grover boys led us off.
They worked a charm,
Baby on the sax,
Jake on the banjo,
and Ben on the clarinet.
The Baker family followed, playing
just like they do at home
every night after dinner.
They didn't look nervous at all.
The tap dancers,
they rattled the teeth in their jaws
and the eyeballs in their skulls,

their feet flying,
their arms swinging,
their mouths gapping.
Then Sunny Lee Hallem
tumbled and leaped onto the stage,
the sweat flying off her,
spotting the Palace floor.
Marsh Worton struggled out,
his accordion leading the way.
George and Agnes Harkins
    ran their fingers over the
strings of their harps,
made you want to look up
    into the heavens for
angels,
but only scenery
and lights
and ropes and sandbags hung overhead,
and then there was me on piano.

I went on somewhere near the backside
    of middle,
getting more and more jittery with each act,
till my time came.
I played "Bye, Bye, Blackbird"
my own way,
messing with the tempo,
and the first part sounded like
I used just my elbows,
but the middle sounded good

and the end,
I forgot I was even playing
in front of the packed Palace Theatre.
I dropped right inside the music and
didn't feel anything
till after
when the clapping started
and that's when I noticed my hands hurting
straight up to my shoulders.
But the applause
made me forget the pain,
the audience roared when I finished,
they came to their feet,
and I got third prize,
one dollar,
while Mad Dog Craddock, singing,
won second,
and Ben Grover
and his crazy clarinet
took first.

The tap dancers pouted into their mirrors,
peeling off their makeup and their smiles.
Birdie Jasper claimed
it was all my fault she didn't win,
that the judges were just being nice
    to a cripple,
but the harpin' Harkins were kind
and the Hazel Hurd Players
wrapped their long arms around me

and said I was swell
and in the sweaty dim chaos backstage
I ignored the pain running up and down
   my arms,
I felt like I was part of something grand.
But they had to give my ribbon
   and my dollar to my
father,
'cause I couldn't hold
anything in my hands.

February 1935

The Piano Player

Arley says,
"We're
doing a show at the school
    in a week, Billie Jo.
Come play with us."

If I asked my father
he'd say yes.
It's okay with him if I want to play.
He didn't even know I was at the piano again
    till the
other night.
He's making some kind of effort
    to get on
better with me now,
Since I "did him proud" at the Palace.

But I say, "No."

It's too soon after the contest.
It still hurts too much.

Arley doesn't understand.
"Just practice more," he says.
"You'll get it back,
you can travel with us again this summer

if you'd like."

I don't say
it hurts like the parched earth
  with each note.
I don't say,
one chord and
my hands scream with pain for days.
I don't show him
the swelling
or my tears.

I tell him, "I'll try."

At home, I sit at
Ma's piano,
I don't touch the keys.
I don't know why.

I play "Stormy Weather" in my mind,
following the phrases in my imagination,
saving strength,
so that when I sit down at a piano
  that is not Ma's,
when everyone crowds into the school
for Arley's show,
no one can say
that Billie Jo Kelby plays like a cripple.

March 1935

No Good

I did play like a cripple at Arley's show,
not that Arley would ever say it.
But my hands are no good anymore,
my playing's no good.
Arley understands, I think.
He won't ask again.

March 1935

Snow

Had to check
yesterday morning
to make sure that was
snow
on the ground,
not dust.
But you can't make a dustball
pack together
and slam against the side of the barn, and
echo across the fields.
So I know
it was snow.

March 1935

Night School

My father thought maybe
he ought to go to night school,
so if the farm failed
there'd be prospects to fall back on.
He's starting to sound like Ma.

"The farm won't fail," I tell him.
"Long as we get some good rain."
I'm starting to sound like him.

"It's mostly ladies in those classes," he says,
"they take bookkeeping and civics,
and something called business English."

I can't imagine him
taking any of those things.
But maybe he doesn't care so much
    about the classes.
Maybe he's thinking more
    about the company of ladies.

I'll bet none of the ladies mind
spending time with my father,
he's still good looking
with his strong back,
and his blondy-red hair

and his high cheeks rugged with wind.

I shouldn't mind either.
It's dinner I don't have to
come up with,
'cause the ladies bring chicken
    and biscuits for him.
I'm glad to get out of cooking.
Sometimes with my hands,
it's hard to keep the fire,
wash the pans,
hold the knife, and spread a little butter.
But I do mind his spending time
    with all those
biddies.

I turn my back on him as he goes,
and settle myself in the parlor
and touch Ma's piano.

My fingers leave sighs
in the dust.

March 1935

Dust Pneumonia

Two Fridays ago,
Pete Guymon drove in with a
truck full of produce.
He joked with Calb Hardly,
Mr. Hardly's son,
while they unloaded eggs and cream
down at the store.
Pete Guymon teased Calb Hardly
  about the Wildcats
losing to Hooker.
Calb Hardly teased Pete Guymon
  about his wheezy truck
sucking in dust.

Last Friday,
Pete Guymon took ill with dust pneumonia.
Nobody knew how to keep
  that produce truck on the
road.
It sat,
filled with turkeys and heavy hens
waiting for delivery,
it sat out in front of Pete's drafty shack,
and sits there still,
the cream curdling
the apples going soft.

Because a couple of hours ago,
Pete Guymon died.
Mr. Hardly
was already on the phone
    to a new produce supplier,
before evening.
He had people in his store
and no food to sell them.

His boy, Calb,
slammed the basketball
    against the side of the house
until Calb's ma yelled for him to quit,
and late that night a truck rattled up
    to the store,
with colored springs,
dozens of hens,
filthy eggs,
and a driver with no interest whatsoever
    in young
Calb Hardly
or his precious Wildcats.

March 1935

Dust Storm

I never would have gone to see the show
if I had known a storm like this would come.
I didn't know when going in,
but coming out
a darker night I'd never seen.
I bumped into a box beside the Palace door
and scraped my shins,
then tripped on something in my path,
I don't know what,
and walked into a phone pole,
bruised my cheek.

The first car that I met was sideways
   in the road.
Bowed down, my eyes near shut,
trying to keep the dust out,
I saw his headlights just before
   I reached them.

The driver called me over and I felt my way,
following his voice.
He asked me how I kept the road.
"I feel it with my feet," I shouted over the
roaring wind,
"I walk along the edge.
One foot on the road, one on the shoulder."

And desperate to get home,
he straightened out his car,
and straddled tires on the road and off,
and slowly pulled away.

I kept along. I know that there were others
on the road,
from time to time I'd hear someone cry out,
their voices rose like ghosts
    on the howling wind;
no one could see. I stopped at neighbors'
just to catch my breath
and made my way from town
out to our farm.
Everyone said to stay
but I guessed
my father would
come out to find me
if I didn't show,
and get himself lost in the
raging dust and maybe die
and I
didn't want that burden on my soul.

Brown earth rained down
from sky.
I could not catch my breath
the way the dust pressed on my chest
and wouldn't stop.
The dirt blew down so thick

it scratched my eyes
and stung my tender skin,
it plugged my nose and
   filled inside my mouth.
No matter how I pressed my lips together,
the dust made muddy tracks
across my tongue.

But I kept on,
spitting out mud,
covering my mouth,
clamping my nose,
the dust stinging the raw and open
stripes of scarring on my hands,
and after some three hours I made it home.

Inside I found my father's note
that said he'd gone to find me
and if I should get home, to just stay put.
I hollered out the front door
and the back;
he didn't hear,
I didn't think he would.
The wind took my voice and busted it
into a thousand pieces,
so small
the sound
blew out over Ma and Franklin's grave,
thinner than a sigh.

I waited for my father through the night,
   coughing up
dust,
cleaning dust out of my ears,
rinsing my mouth,
   blowing mud out of my nose.

Joe De La Flor stopped by around four
   to tell me
they found one boy tangled
   in a barbed-wire fence,
another smothered in a drift of dust.

After Joe left I thought
   of the famous Lindberghs,
and how their baby was killed
   and never came back
to them.
I wondered if my father would come back.

He blew in around six a.m.
It hurt,
the sight of him
brown with dirt,
his eyes as red as raw meat,
his feet bruised from walking in worn shoes
stepping where he couldn't see
on things that bit and cut into his flesh.

I tried to scare up something we could eat,
but couldn't keep the table clear of dust.
Everything I set
down for our breakfast
was covered before we took a bite,
and so we chewed the grit and swallowed
and I thought of the cattle
dead from mud in their lungs,
and I thought of the tractor
buried up to the steering wheel,
and Pete Guymon,
and I couldn't even recognize the man
sitting across from me,
sagging in his chair,
his red hair gray and stiff with dust,
his face deep lines of dust,
his teeth streaked brown with dust.
I turned the plates and glasses upside down,
crawled into bed, and slept.

March 1935

Broken Promise

It rained
a little
everywhere
but here.

March 1935

Motherless

If Ma could put her arm
   across my shoulder
sometime,
or stroke back my hair,
or sing me to sleep, making the soft sounds,
the reassuring noises,
that no matter how brittle
   and sharp life seemed,
no matter how brittle and sharp she seemed,
she was still my ma who loved me,
then I think I wouldn't be so eager to go.

March 1935

Following in His Steps

Haydon Parley Nye's wife,
Fonda,
died today,
two months after she lost her man.

The cause of death was
dust pneumonia,
but I think
she couldn't go on without Haydon.

When Ma died,
I didn't want to go on, either.
I don't know. I don't feel the same now,
not exactly.
Now that I see that one day
comes after another
and you get through them
one measure at a time.
But I'd like to go,
not like Fonda Nye,
I don't want to die,
I just want to go,
away,
out of the dust.

March 1935

Spring 1935

Heartsick

The hard part is in spite of everything
if I had any boy court me,
it'd be Mad Dog Craddock.
But Mad Dog can have any girl.
Why would he want me?

I'm so restless.
My father asks what's going on with me.
I storm up to my room,
leaving him alone
standing in the kitchen.
If Ma was here
she would come up and listen.
And then later,
she would curl beside my father,
and assure him that everything was all right,
and soothe him into his farmer's sleep.

My father and I,
we can't soothe each other.
I'm too young,
he's too old,
and we don't know how to talk anymore
if we ever did.

April 1935

Skin

My father has a raised spot
on the side of his nose
that never was there before
and won't go away.
And there's another on his cheek
and two more on his neck,
and I wonder
why the heck is he fooling around.
He knows what it is.
His father had those spots too.

April 1935

Regrets

I never go by Arley's anymore.
Still,
every week
he comes to school to teach and
sometimes
I bump into Vera, or
Miller Rice,
or Mad Dog.

They are always kind.
They ask after my father.
They ask how my hands are feeling.
I cross my arms in front of me
tight
so my scars won't show.

These days Mad Dog looks at me
halfway between picking a fight
    and kindness.
He walks with me a ways some afternoons,
never says a word.
He's quiet once the other girls go off.
I've had enough of quiet men.
I ought to keep clear of Mad Dog.
But I don't.

April 1935

Fire on the Rails

I hate fire.
Hate it.
But the entire Oklahoma Panhandle
   is so dry,
everything is going up in flames.
Everything too ready to ignite.
Last week
the school caught fire.
Damage was light,
on account of it being caught early.
Most kids joked about it next day,
but it terrified me.
I could hardly go back in the building.
And this week
three boxcars
in the train yard
burned to ash.
Jim Goin and Harry Kesler
spotted the fire,
and that was a miracle
considering the fierceness of the dust storm
at the time.
The fire boys
tore over,
but they couldn't put the blaze out
   without water,

and water is exactly what they didn't have.
So they separated the burning cars
and moved them down a siding,
away from any little thing that might catch
if the flames hopped.
It was all they talked about at school.
The dust blew,
they say,
so you'd think it would have smothered
   the fire out,
but the flames,
crazy in the wind,
licked away at the wooden frames
   of the three box
cars,
until nothing remained but warped metal,
and twisted rails,
scorched dirt, and
charred ties.

No one talks about fire
right to my face.
They can't forget how fire changed my life.
But I hear them talking anyway.

April 1935

The Mail Train

They promised
through rain,
heat,
snow,
and gloom
but they never said anything about dust.

And so the mail got stuck
for hours,
for days,
on the Santa Fe
because mountains of dust
had blown over the tracks,
because blizzards of dust
blocked the way.

And all that time,
as the dust beat down on the cars,
a letter was waiting inside a mail bag.
A letter from Aunt Ellis, my father's sister,
written just to me,
inviting me to live with her in Lubbock.
I want to get out of here,
but not to Aunt Ellis,
and not to Lubbock, Texas.
My father didn't say much when I asked

what I should do.
"Let's wait and see,"
he said.
What's that supposed to mean?

April 1935

Migrants

We'll be back when the rain comes,
they say,
pulling away with all they own,
straining the springs of their motor cars.
Don't forget us.

And so they go,
fleeing the blowing dust,
fleeing the fields of brown-tipped wheat
barely ankle high,
and sparse as the hair on a dog's belly.

We'll be back, they say,
pulling away toward Texas,
Arkansas,
where they can rent a farm,
pull in enough cash,
maybe start again.

We'll be back when it rains,
they say,
setting out with their bedsprings
    and mattresses,
their cookstoves and dishes,
their kitchen tables,
and their milk goats

tied to their running boards
in rickety cages,
setting out for
California,
where even though they say
　they'll come back,
they just might stay
if what they hear about that place is true.

Don't forget us, they say.
But there are so many leaving,
how can I remember them all?

April 1935

Blankets of Black

On the first clear day
we staggered out of our caves of dust
into the sunlight,
turning our faces to the big blue sky.

On the second clear day
we believed
the worst was over at last.
We flocked outside,
traded in town,
going to stores and coming out
only to find the air still clear
and gentle,
grateful for each easy breath.

On the third clear day
summer came in April
and the churches opened their arms
   to all comers
and all comers came.
After church,
folks headed for
picnics,
car trips. No one could stay inside.

My father and I argued about the funeral

of Grandma Lucas,
who truly was no relation.
But we ended up going anyway,
driving down the road in a procession
   to Texhoma.

Six miles out of town the air turned cold,
birds beat their wings
everywhere you looked,
whole flocks
dropping out of the sky,
crowding on fence posts.
I was sulking in the truck beside my father
when
heaven's shadow crept across the plains,
a black cloud,
big and silent as Montana,
boiling on the horizon and
barreling toward us.
More birds tumbled from the sky
frantically keeping ahead of the dust.

We watched as the storm
   swallowed the light.
The sky turned from blue
to black,
night descended in an instant
and the dust was on us.

The wind screamed.

171

The blowing dirt ran
so thick
I couldn't see the brim of my hat
as we plunged from the truck,
fleeing.

The dust swarmed
like it had never swarmed before.

My father groped for my hand,
pulled me away from the truck.
We ran,
a blind pitching toward the shelter
    of a small house,
almost invisible,
our hands tight together,
running toward the ghostly door,
pounding on it with desperation.

A woman opened her home to us,
all of us,
not just me and my father,
but the entire funeral procession,
and one after another,
we tumbled inside, gasping,
our lungs burning for want of air.

All the lamps were lit against the dark,
the house dazed by dust,
gazed weakly out.

The walls shook in the howling wind.
We helped tack up sheets
   on the windows and doors
to keep the dust down.

Cars and trucks
unable to go on,
their ignitions shorted out
   by the static electricity,
opened up and let out more passengers,
who stumbled for shelter.
One family came in
clutched together,
their pa, divining the path
with a long wooden rod.

If it hadn't been for the company,
this storm would have broken us
completely,
broken us more thoroughly than
the plow had broken the Oklahoma sod,
more thoroughly than my burns
had broken the ease of my hands.
But for the sake of the crowd,
and the hospitality of the home
   that sheltered us,
we held on
and waited,
sitting or standing, breathing
   through wet cloths

as the fog of dust filled the room
and settled slowly over us.

When it let up a bit,
some went on to bury Grandma Lucas,
but my father and I,
we cleaned the thick layer of grime
off the truck,
pulled out of the procession
    and headed on home,
creeping slowly
    along the dust-mounded road.

When we got back,
we found the barn half covered in dunes,
I couldn't tell which rise of dust was Ma and
Franklin's grave.
The front door hung open,
blown in by the wind.
Dust lay two feet deep in ripply waves
across the parlor floor,
dust blanketed the cookstove,
the icebox,
the kitchen chairs,
everything deep in dust.
And the piano . . .
buried in dust.

While I started to shovel,
my father went out to the barn.

174

He came back, and when I asked, he said
the animals
weren't good,
and the tractor was dusted out,
and I said, "It's a wonder
the truck got us home."
I should have held my tongue.
When he tried starting the truck again,
it wouldn't turn over.

April 1935

The Visit

Mad Dog came by
to see how we made out
after the duster.

He didn't come to court me.
I didn't think he had.

We visited more than an hour.
The sky cleared enough to see Black Mesa.
I showed him my father's pond.

Mad Dog said he was going to Amarillo,
to sing, on the radio,
and if he sang good enough,
they might give him a job there.

"You'd leave the farm?" I asked.
He nodded.
"You'd leave school?"
He shrugged.

Mad Dog scooped a handful of dust,
like a boy in a sandpit.
He said, "I love this land,
no matter what."
I looked at his hands.

They were scarless.

Mad Dog stayed longer than he planned.
He ran down the road
back to his father's farm
    when he realized the time.
Dust rose each place his foot fell,
leaving a trace of him
long after he'd gone.

April 1935

Freak Show

The fellow from Canada,
James Kingsbury,
photographer from the *Toronto Star*,
way up there in Ontario,
the man who took the first pictures of
the Dionne Quintuplets,
left his homeland and
came to Joyce City
looking for some other piece of
oddness,
hoping to photograph the drought
and the dust storms
and
he did
with the help of Bill Rotterdaw
and Handy Poole,
who took him to the sandiest farms and
showed off the boniest cattle in the county.

Mr. Kingsbury's pictures
   of those Dionne babies
got them famous,
but it also got them taken from their
mother and father
and put on display
like a freak show,

like a tent full of two-headed calves.
Now I'm wondering
what will happen to us
after he finishes taking pictures of our dust.

April 1935

Help from Uncle Sam

The government
is lending us money
to keep the farm going,
money to buy seed,
feed loans for our cow,
for our mule,
for the chickens still alive and the hog,
as well as a little bit of feed
for us.

My father was worried about
paying back,
because of what Ma had said,
but Mrs. Love,
the lady from FERA,
assured him he didn't need
   to pay a single cent
until the crops came in,
and if the crops never came,
   then he wouldn't pay a
thing.

So my father said
okay.
Anything to keep going.
He put the paperwork on the shelf,

beside Ma's book of poetry
and the invitation from Aunt Ellis.
He just keeps that invitation from her,
glowering down at me from the shelf
   above the piano.

April 1935

Let Down

I was invited to graduation,
to play the piano.

I couldn't play.
It had been too long.
My hands wouldn't work.
I just sat on the piano bench,
staring down at the keys.
Everyone waited.
When the silence went on so long
folks started to whisper,
Arley Wanderdale lowered his head and
Miss Freeland started to cry.
I don't know,
I let them down.

I didn't cry.
Too stubborn.
I got up and walked off the stage.

I thought maybe if my father ever went
    to Doc Rice
to do something about the spots on his skin,
Doc could check my hands too,
tell me what to do about them.

But my father isn't going to Doc Rice,
and now
I think we're both turning to dust.

May 1935

Hope

It started out as snow,
oh,
big flakes
floating
softly,
catching on my sweater,
lacy on the edges of my sleeves.

Snow covered the dust,
softened the
fences,
soothed the parched lips
of the land.

And then it changed,
halfway between snow and rain,
sleet,
glazing the earth.

Until at last
it slipped into rain,
light as mist.

It was the kindest
kind of rain
that fell.

Soft and then a little heavier,
helping along
what had already fallen
into the
hard-pan
earth
until it
rained,
steady as a good friend
who walks beside you,
not getting in your way,
staying with you through a hard time.

And because the rain came
so patient and slow at first,
and built up strength as the earth
remembered how to yield,
instead of washing off,
the water slid in,
into the dying ground
and softened its stubborn pride,
and eased it back toward life.

And then,
just when we thought it would end,
after three such gentle days,
the rain
came
slamming down,
tons of it,

soaking into the ready earth
to the primed and greedy earth,
and soaking deep.

It kept coming,
thunder booming,
lightning
kicking,
dancing from the heavens
down to the prairie,
and my father
dancing with it,
dancing outside in the drenching night
with the gutters racing,
with the earth puddled and pleased,
with my father's near-finished pond filling.

When the rain stopped,
my father splashed out to the barn,
and spent
two days and two nights
cleaning dust out of his tractor,
until he got it running again.
In the dark, headlights shining,
he idled toward the freshened fields,
certain the grass would grow again,
certain the weeds would grow again,
certain the wheat would grow again too.

May 1935

The Rain's Gift

The rain
has brought back some grass
and the ranchers
have put away the
feed cake
and sent their cattle
out to graze.
Joe De La Flor
is singing in his saddle again.

May 1935

Hope Smothered

While I washed up dinner dishes in the pan,
the wind came from the west
bringing —
dust.
I'd just stripped all the gummed tape
    from the
windows.
Now I've got dust all over the clean dishes.

I can hardly make myself
get started cleaning again.

Mrs. Love is taking applications
for boys to do CCC work.
Any boy between eighteen
    and twenty-eight can join.
I'm too young
and the wrong sex
but what I wouldn't give to be
working for the CCC
somewhere far from here,
out of the dust.

May 1935

Sunday Afternoon
at the Amarillo Hotel

Everybody gathered at
the Joyce City Hardware
   and Furniture Company
on Sunday
to hear Mad Dog Craddock
sing on WDAG
from the Amarillo Hotel.
They hooked up speakers
and the sweet sound
of Mad Dog's voice
filled the creaky aisles.

Arley Wanderdale was in Amarillo
   with Mad Dog,
singing and playing the piano,
and the Black Mesa Boys were there
too.
I ached for not being there with them.

But there was nothing more most folks
   in Joyce City
wanted to do
than spend a half hour
leaning on counters,
sitting on stairs,

189

resting in chairs,
staring at the hardware
and the tableware,
listening to hometown boys
making big-time music
on the radio.

They kept time in the aisles,
hooting after each number,
and when Mad Dog finished his last song,
   they sent
the dust swirling,
cheering and whooping,
patting each other on the back,
as if they'd been featured
on WDAG themselves.

I tried cheering for Mad Dog
   with everyone else,
but my throat
felt like a trap had
snapped down on it.

That Mad Dog, he didn't have
a thing to worry about.
He sang good, all right.
He'll go far as he wants.

May 1935

Baby

Funny thing about babies.
Ma died having one,
the Lindberghs said good night to one
   and lost it,
and somebody
last Saturday
decided to
give one away.

Reverend Bingham says
that Harley Madden
was sweeping the dust out of church,
shining things up for Sunday service,
when he swept himself up to a package
on the north front steps.

He knelt,
studying the parcel,
and called to Reverend Bingham,
who came right by
   and opened the package up.

It held a living baby.
Reverend Bingham took it to Doc Rice.
Doc checked it, said it was fine,
only small,

less than a five-pound sack of sugar,
and a little cold from
spending time on the north front steps,
but Mrs. Bingham
and the reverend
warmed that baby with
blankets and sugar water,
and tender talk,
and the whole of Joyce City
    came forward with gifts.

I asked my father if we could adopt it,
but he said
we stood about as much chance
of getting that baby
as the wheat stood of growing,
since we couldn't give the baby anything
not even a ma.
Then he looked at me
sorry as dust.
And to make up for it,
he pulled out a box
    with the rest of the clothes
Ma had made for our new baby
and told me to drop them
    by the church if I wanted.

I found the dimes Ma'd been saving,
my earnings from the piano,
inside an envelope,

in the box of baby Franklin's nighties.
She had kept those dimes to send me
to Panhandle A and M.
To study music.

No point now.

I sat at her piano a long time after I
got back from the church,
imagining
a song for my little brother,
buried in Ma's arms on a knoll
   overlooking the
banks of the Beaver,
imagining a song for the Lindbergh baby
stiff in the woods,
imagining a song for this new baby
who
would not be my father's son.

May 1935

Old Bones

Once
dinosaurs roamed
in Cimarron County.
Bones
showing
in the green shale,
ribs the size of plow blades,
hip bones like crank phones,
and legs running
like fence rails
down to a giant
foot.

A chill shoots up my spine
imagining a dinosaur
slogging out of an Oklahoma sea,
with turtles swimming around its legs.
I can see it sunning itself
    on the swampy banks,
beyond it a forest of ferns.
It's almost easy to imagine,
gazing out from our house
at the dust-crushed fields,
easy to imagine filling
    in all the emptiness with green,
easy to imagine such a beast

brushing an itchy rump against our barn.
But all that remains of it
is bone,
broken and turned to stone,
trapped in the hillside,
this once-upon-a-time real-live dinosaur
who lived,
and fed,
and roamed
like a ridiculous
long-necked cow,
and then fell down and died.
I think for a moment of Joe De La Flor
herding brontosaurus instead of cattle
and I
smile.

I tell my father,
Let's go to the site
and watch the men chip away with ice picks,
let's see how they plaster the bones.
Please, before they ship the whole thing
    to Norman.

I am thinking
that a dinosaur is getting out of Joyce City
a hundred million years too late to
appreciate the trip,
and that I ought to get out before my own
bones turn to stone.

But I keep my thoughts to myself.

My father thinks awhile,
rubbing that spot on his neck.
He looks out the window,
out across the field,
toward the knoll where Ma and the baby lie.
"It's best to let the dead rest," he says.
And we stay home.

June 1935

Summer 1935

The Dream

Piano, my silent
    mother,
        I can touch you,
you are cool
    and smooth
        and willing
to stay with me
    stay with me
        talk to me.
Uncomplaining
    you accept
        the cover to your keys
and still
    you
        make room
for all that I
    place
        there.

We close our eyes
    together
        and together find that stillness
like a pond
    a pond
        when the wind is quiet
and the surface

glazes
    gazing unblinking
at the blue sky.
    I play songs
        that have only the pattern
of my self in them
    and you hum along
        supporting me.
You are the
    companion
        to myself.
The mirror
    with my mother's eyes.

July 1935

Midnight Truth

I am so filled with bitterness,
it comes from the dust, it comes
from the silence of my father, it comes
from the absence of Ma.

I could've loved her better.
She could've loved me, too.
But she's rock and dust and wind now,
she's carved stone,
she's holding my stone brother.

I have given my father so many chances
to understand, to
reach out, to
love me. He once did.
I remember his smile,
his easy talk.
Now there's nothing easy between us.
Sometimes he takes notice of me,
like coming after me in the dust.
But mostly I'm invisible.
Mostly I'm alone.

My father's digging his own grave,
he calls it a pond,
but I know what he's up to.

He is rotting away,
like his father,
ready to leave me behind in the dust.
Well, I'm leaving first.

July 1935

Out of the Dust

This is not a dream.
There's no comfort in dreams.
I try to contain the ache as I leave my bed,
I try to still my heart as I
slip from my room with my kerchief
    of dimes.
Moving slowly down the stairs,
I cross through the kitchen,
    taking only some
biscuits,
and leave my father's house.
It's the middle of the night
    and I hear every sound
inside me, outside me.
I go,
knowing that I'll die if I stay,
that I'm slowly, surely
smothering.

I walk through the calm night,
under the stars.
I walk to
where the train stops long enough
for a long-legged girl to latch on
and as my heart races
I feel the earth tremble beneath me and then

the sound of sharp knives,
metal against metal,
as the train pulls up to the station.

Once I might've headed east,
to Mr. Roosevelt.
Now I slip under cover of darkness
inside a boxcar
and let the train carry me west.
Out of the dust.

August 1935

Gone West

I am stiff and sore.
In two endless days on this train, I have
burned in the desert,
shivered in the mountains,
I have seen the
camps of dust-bowl migrants
along the tracks.

There was one girl.
I saw her through the slat in the boxcar.
She stared up at the passing train.
She stood by the tracks watching,
and I knew her.

August 1935

Something Lost, Something Gained

He climbs into my car.
He's dirty and he has a sour smell.
His eyes are ringed by the soil that comes
    from riding
trains.
But there's a deeper shadow to those eyes,
like ashes,
like death.
He needs a hair comb and a shave,
and a mending needle applied to his pants.

He speaks to me,
"Where you from, miss?" he wants to know.
He shows me a picture of his family.
A wife. Three boys.
The photograph is all he carries.
That and the shredding, stinking clothes
    on his back.
I feed him two of the stale biscuits
    I've been hoarding
and save the rest.
I'll be hungry tonight,
what with giving my day's biscuits away.
But I can see the gaunt of hunger
    in his cheeks.
He asks if I have water and I shake my head,

my tongue thick with thirst.
He eats the biscuits.
He doesn't care they're caked with dust.
He finishes eating and crumbs
   stick to his mustache.
He's staring hard at me and his eyes water.
"I've done it again," he says.
"Taken food from a child."
I show him my cloth bag with more biscuits.
"At home," he said, "I couldn't feed them,
couldn't stand the baby always crying.
And my wife,
always that dark look following me.
Couldn't take no more.

Lost our land, they tractored us out
   so's we had to
leave,
rented awhile, then moved
   in with Lucille's kin.
Couldn't make nothing grow."

I nodded. "I know."

We talked as the train rocked,
as the cars creaked,
as the miles showed nothing
   but empty space,
we talked through the pink
   of the setting sun,

and into the dark.
I told him about Ma dying.
I told him about my father,
and how the thing that scared us both
    the most
was being left alone.
And now I'd gone and left him.
I told him about the piano,
and Arley Wanderdale,
and how I wasn't certain of the date,
but I thought it might be my birthday,
but he was sleeping by then, I think.

He was like tumbleweed.
Ma had been tumbleweed too,
holding on for as long as she could,
then blowing away on the wind.

My father was more like the sod.
Steady, silent, and deep.
Holding on to life, with reserves underneath
to sustain him, and me,
and anyone else who came near.
My father
stayed rooted, even with my tests
    and my temper,
even with the double sorrow of
his grief and my own,
he had kept a home
until I broke it.

When I woke,
the man was gone, and so were my biscuits,
but under my hat I found
the photograph of his
family,
the wife and three boys.
Maybe the photograph was
left in trade for the biscuits,
maybe it was a birthday gift,
the one thing he had left to give.
The children in the picture
were clean and serious,
looking out with a certain longing.
The baby had his eyes.
On the back of the photograph,
in pencil,
was the address of his family in
Moline, Kansas.
First chance, I'd send the picture back,
let his wife know he was still alive.

I got off the train in Flagstaff, Arizona.
A lady from a government agency saw me.
She gave me water and food.
I called Mr. Hardly from her office
and asked him to
let my father know . . .
I was coming home.

August 1935

Homeward Bound

Getting away,
it wasn't any better.
Just different.
And lonely.
Lonelier than the wind.
Emptier than the sky.
More silent than the dust,
piled in drifts between me
and my
father.

August 1935

Met

My father is waiting at the station
and I call him
Daddy
for the first time
since Ma died,
and we walk home,
together,
talking.
I tell him about getting out of the dust
and how I can't get out of something
that's inside me.
I tell him he is like the sod,
and I am like the wheat,
and I can't grow everywhere,
but I can grow here,
with a little rain,
with a little care,
with a little luck.
And I tell him how scared I am
    about those spots on
his skin
and I see he's scared too.
"I can't be my own mother," I tell him,
"and I can't be my own father
and if you're both going to leave me,
well,

what am I supposed to do?"
And when I tell Daddy so,
he promises to call Doc Rice.

He says the pond is done.
We can swim in it once it fills,
and he'll stock it with fish too,
catfish, that I can go out and
catch of an evening
and fry up.
He says I can even plant flowers,
if I want.

As we walk together,
side by side,
in the swell of dust,
I am forgiving him, step by step,
for the pail of kerosene.
As we walk together,
side by side,
in the sole-deep dust,
I am forgiving myself
for all the rest.

August 1935

Autumn 1935

Cut It Deep

I went in with Daddy to see Doc Rice.
Doc said,
"Why'd you wait so long
to show someone those spots, Bayard?"
I scowled at Daddy.
He looked at the wall.
I think
he didn't care much,
if he had some cancer
and took and died.
Figured he'd see Ma then,
he'd see my brother.
It'd be out of his hands.
He'd be out of the dust.

Now he's going to wear bandages
where Doc cut the cancer out
the best he could.
And we have to wait
and hope Daddy didn't
get help too late.

I ask Doc about my hands.
"What," I say,
"can I do with them?"
Doc looks carefully at the mottled skin,

the stretched and striped and crackled skin.
"Quit picking at them," he says.
"Rub some ointment in them
   before you go to bed,"
he says.
"And use them, Billie Jo," he says.
"They'll heal up fine if you just use them."

Daddy sits on my bed
and I open the boxes,
the two boxes
that have been in my closet
for years now.
The dust is over everything,
but I blow it off,
and Daddy is so quiet
when he sees
some of the things
that're still so strong of Ma,
and we end up
   keeping everything but a palmful
of broken doll dishes.
I thought once to go through
   these boxes with
Ma,
but Daddy is
sitting on the edge of my bed.
My mouth feels cottony.
I fix dinner
and Daddy tells me about

when he was a boy.
He says, "I wasn't always sure
about the wheat,
about the land,
about life in the Panhandle.
I dreamed of running off too,
though I never did.
I didn't have half your sauce,
  Billie Jo," he says.
And it's the first time I ever knew
there was so much to the two of us,
so much more than our red hair
and our long legs
and the way we rub our eyes
when we're tired.

October 1935

The Other Woman

Her name is Louise,
she stayed by Daddy the days I was away.

The first time I met her
    she came to dinner bringing two
baskets of food.
She's a good cook
without showing off.

She has a way of making my father
    do things.
When Louise came to dinner,
Daddy got up and cleaned the kitchen
    when we were
done eating.
He tied an apron around his middle
and he looked silly as a cow
stuck in a hole,
but Louise ignored that,
and I took a lesson from her.

We walked around the farm
even though she'd probably already seen it
while I was gone.
She didn't ask to be taken to
    my favorite places,

the loft in the barn,
the banks of the Beaver,
the field where you can
see Black Mesa on a clear day.
She told me
she knew Daddy and I had a history
    before her,
and she wished she'd been there
    for the whole thing,
but she wasn't and there wasn't anything
    to do
but get over it and get on.

We both stared in wonder
at the pond my daddy made
and she said,
a hole like that says a lot about a man.

I didn't intend to, but I liked her,
because she was so plain and so honest,
and because she made Daddy laugh,
and me, too, just like that,
and even though I didn't know
if there was room for her
in me, I could see there was room
    for her in Daddy.
When I asked him if he wanted me
to go off to Aunt Ellis after all,
Daddy said he hadn't ever wanted it,
he said I was his own and he didn't like to

think about what Aunt Ellis
   might do with me.
And we laughed,
   picturing me and Aunt Ellis
together,
and it wasn't a nice laugh, but it was
Aunt Ellis we were talking about after all.

The thing about Louise,
I'll just have to watch how things go
   and hope
she doesn't crowd me out of Daddy's life,
   not now,
when I am just finding my way back into it.

October 1935

Not Everywhere

I walk with Daddy
up the slope and look out
   over the Beaver River.
Louise is back at the house.
She wanted to come
but this is Ma's place,
Ma's grave,
Franklin's too,
and Louise has no business here.
She wants to come everywhere with us.
Well, I won't let her.
Not everywhere.

Daddy says,
"She could have come.
There's room enough for everyone,
   Billie Jo."
But there's not.
She can come into Ma's kitchen.
She can hang around the barn.
She can sit beside Daddy
   when he drives the truck.
But Ma's bones are in this hill,
Ma's and Franklin's.
And their bones wouldn't like it,
if Louise came walking up here between us.

October 1935

My Life, or What I Told Louise After the Tenth Time She Came to Dinner

"I may look like Daddy,
   but I have my mother's
hands.
Piano hands, Ma called them,
sneaking a look at them any chance she got.
A piano is a grand thing," I say.
"Though ours is covered in dust now.
Under the grime it's dark brown,
like my mother's eyes."

I think about the piano
and how above it hangs a mirror
and to either side of that mirror,
shelves,
where Ma and Daddy's wedding picture
   once stood,
though Daddy has taken that down.

"Whenever she could,
Ma filled a bowl with apples," I tell Louise.
"I'm crazy about apples,
and she filled a jar with wildflowers
   when she
found them,

and put them on that shelf above the piano."

On the other shelf Ma's book of poetry
    remains.
And the invitation from Aunt Ellis,
or what's left of it.
Daddy and I tore it into strips
to mark the poems we thought
    Ma liked best.

"We weren't always happy," I tell Louise.
"But we were happy enough
until the accident.
When I rode the train west,
I went looking for something,
but I didn't see anything wonderful.
I didn't see anything better
    than what I already had.
Home."

I look straight into Louise's face.
Louise doesn't flinch.
She looks straight back.
I am the first one to back down.

"My hands don't look real pretty anymore.
But they hardly hurt. They only ache a little,
sometimes.
I could play right now,
maybe,

if I could get the dust out of the piano,
if I wanted to get the dust out of the piano.
But I don't. I'm not ready yet."

And what I like best about her,
is Louise doesn't say what I should do.
She just nods.
And I know she's heard everything I said,
and some things I didn't say too.

November 1935

November Dust

The wheat is growing
even though dust
blows in sometimes.

I walk with Daddy around the farm
and see that
the pond is holding its own,
it will keep Ma's apple trees alive,
nourish her garden,
help the grass around it grow,
enough to lie in and dream
if I feel like it,
and stand in,
and wait for Mad Dog
when he comes past once a week
on his way from Amarillo,
where he works for the radio.

And as long as the
dust doesn't crush
the winter wheat,
we'll have something to show in the spring
for all Daddy's hard work.
Not a lot, but more than last year.

November 1935

Thanksgiving List

Prairie birds, the whistle of gophers,
   the wind
blowing,
the smell of grass
and spicy earth,
friends like Mad Dog,
   the cattle down in the river,
water washing over their hooves,
the sky so
big, so full of
shifting clouds,
the cloud shadows creeping
over the fields,
Daddy's smile,
and his laugh,
and his songs,
Louise,
food without dust,
Daddy seeing to Ma's piano,
newly cleaned and tuned,
the days when my hands don't hurt at all,
the thank-you note
   from Lucille in Moline, Kansas,
the sound of rain,
Daddy's hole staying full of water
as the windmill turns,

the smell of green,
of damp earth,
of hope returning to our farm.
The poppies set to
bloom on Ma and Franklin's grave,
the morning with the whole day waiting,
full of promise,
the night
of quiet, of no expectations, of rest.
And the certainty of home, the one I live in,
and the one
that lives in me.

November 1935

Music

I'm getting to know the music again.
And it is getting to know me.
We sniff each other's armpits,
and inside each other's ears,
and behind each other's necks.
We are both confident, and a little sassy.

And I know now that all the time
    I was trying to get
out of the dust,
the fact is,
what I am,
I am because of the dust.
And what I am is good enough.
Even for me.

November 1935

Teamwork

Louise and I take walks after dinner
every time she comes.
By the time we get back
the kitchen looks pretty good,
Daddy only leaves a few things he doesn't
understand,
like big pans,
and wooden spoons,
and leftovers,
and that makes me a little irritated
but mostly it makes me love him.
And Louise, knowing exactly what's left
    to be done,
helps me finish up.

She was my father's teacher
    at the night school class.
She never married.
She went to college for two years
and studied and worked,
and didn't notice how lonely she was
until she met Daddy and fell into the
big hurt of his eyes.
She knows how to keep a home,
she knows how to cook,
she knows how to make things

last through winters
and drought.
She knows how to smooth things
  between two
redheaded people.
And she knows how to come into a home
and not step on the toes of a ghost.
I still feel grateful
  she didn't make cranberry sauce
last month, at the first Thanksgiving we
spent together.
Louise made sweet potatoes
  and green beans,
and turkey, and two pies, pumpkin
and chocolate.
I was so full
my lids
sighed shut and Daddy walked
  with Louise instead of
me
out to Ma and Franklin's grave,
where he let Ma know his intentions.
And Ma's bones didn't object.
Neither did mine.

And when they came back to the house,
Daddy still cleaned the kitchen.

December 1935

Finding a Way

Daddy
started talking
about planting
the rest of the acres in wheat,
but then said, No,
let's just go with what we've got right now.

And I've
been playing
a half hour
every day,
making the skin stretch,
making the scars stretch.

The way I see it, hard times aren't only
about money,
or drought,
or dust.
Hard times are about losing spirit,
and hope,
and what happens when dreams dry up.

The tractor's busted,
we don't have the cash to fix it,
but there's nothing saying
   Daddy can't do the work

by hand.
It can't be any harder than digging a hole
forty by sixty by six feet deep.

Daddy bought a second mule
    with Louise's help.
Her betrothal gift to him.
He walks behind the team,
step by step, listing the fields
    to fight the wind.
Maybe the tractor lifted him above the land,
maybe the fields didn't know him anymore,
didn't remember the touch of his feet,
or the stroke of his hand,
or the bones of his knees,
and why should wheat grow for a stranger?
Daddy said he'd try some sorghum,
maybe some cotton,
admitting as how there might be something
to this notion of diversification folks were
talking about,
and yes, he'd bring the grass back
like Ma wanted,
where he wasn't planting anything else.
He'd make new sod.
And I'm learning, watching Daddy,
    that you can stay
in one place
and still grow.

I wipe dust out of the roasting pan,
I wipe dust off Ma's dishes,
and wait for Daddy to drive in with Louise,
hoping she'll stay a little later,
a little longer,
waiting for the day when she stays for good.

She wears a comical hat, with flowers,
in December,
and when she smiles,
her face is
full enough of springtime, it makes
her hat seem just right.
She brings apples in a sack,
perfect apples she arranges
in a bowl on the shelf,
opposite the book of poetry.
Sometimes, while I'm at the piano,
I catch her reflection in the mirror,
standing in the kitchen, soft-eyed,
    while Daddy
finishes chores,
and I stretch my fingers over the keys,
and I play.

December 1935

About the Author

Karen Hesse is the author of ten books for children, among them *The Music of Dolphins*, which was named a Best Book of 1996 by both *Publishers Weekly* and *School Library Journal.*

Ms. Hesse lives with her husband and two daughters in Williamsville, Vermont.